Norris the Seahorse Takes on the Bullies

JAIME AMOR

A  YOGA ADVENTURE

W

WATKINS

Sharing Wisdom Since
1893

Today we are off to meet Norris the seahorse
who lives deep in the ocean. Wow!

Just copy the moves in the pictures
and enjoy the adventure.

Let's get ready . . .

Someone's coming on the journey with you!
Can you find Coco the crab hiding
in every picture?

Sit on the floor and cross your legs. Bring your hands together in front of your heart.

Now bow forward and say our yoga code word, "Na-ma-stay", which joins us all together.

Namaste!
Hello!

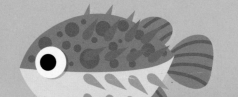

We're going to look for Norris in the sea, so let's make our spines strong for swimming with some special animal **stretches**.

Stretch like a cat! Get up on your hands and knees. Arch your back and look at your belly button.

Meow!

Then dip your belly down and lift your chest. Wiggle waggle your tail, making a happy cat meow.

Now stretch like a dog! Press your feet and hands into the floor and lift your bottom to the sky, going, "Woof, woof, woof!"

Woof!

Woof!

Woof!

Curl up like a mouse. Kneel down and rest your head on the ground. Lay your arms down by your sides.

Now we are ready to go! But before we leave, let's give everyone at home a great big **hug** goodbye.

Come up on your knees and stretch your arms wide.

Then wrap them around your shoulders in a nice, big hug.

Oh! Look who has just landed . . .

It's a rather magical-looking bird
with huge, webbed, blue feet!
It's Bez the blue-footed booby!
He's going to give us a ride to
the beach so we can start looking
for Norris.

We climb onto Bez's feathery back. He
points his **wings** down, then he
swoops up into the sky. We are off!

We fly off over the trees and the hills.

Fly like a bird.
Fold forward,
keeping your back
straight and long.
Stretch your arms out
wide like wings.

6

Gently flap your wings down to the ground and then back up. Pull in your tummy to support your back.

Flap your wings 3 times and then soar on the wind . . . Hold your arms out wide for a moment. Then start flapping them again. Repeat 3 times.

Soon we can see the glittering, blue sea.

Bez starts to fly down and comes to **land** gently on the beach.

Curl up into a ball. Kneel down, fold forward and tuck your arms down behind you.

We climb off Bez's back and he flies off.

See you later, Bez!

It's time to get in the water! We're going to catch a ride with Popcorn the **dolphin**.

Look, there she is!
Popcorn is a great swimmer and loves playing.

To swim like a dolphin, kneel upright, hold your arms out and criss-cross your fingers.

Now drop down on your elbows and rock backward and forward. Make happy clicking dolphin noises.

Click click click click

Popcorn leaps and dives, splashing through the clear, blue water. She's going to take us down to the bottom of the ocean.

Click click click click

The water is lovely and warm and swimming with Popcorn is a lot of fun.

Popcorn dives down deep into the ocean. It's amazing down here! There are forests of seaweed, with long strands of feathery fronds that waft gently from side to side.

Popcorn leaves us on the ocean floor. We are going to **swim** through the seaweed to find Norris's house.

Come onto your tummy to swim through the seaweed. Stretch your arms in front of you.

Lift your feet, arms and head off the ground. Bend your legs up behind you and open your arms wide with each stroke.

At last we reach Norris's **house**.
But where is he?

Let's make a house. Jump your feet wide and point your toes forward to give your house a good, strong base.

Stretch your arms wide and then lift them above your head. Bring your hands together to make a pointy roof.

What's that noise? Someone's coming out of the house and it sounds like they are singing . . .

Seabed Cottage

Hello, Norris!

NORRIS'S SONG I love being me!

My name is Norris, I'm a tiny little fellow
But my nose is long and my body is all yellow.
I rock like a rocking horse gliding through the sea
And I will tell you now that I love being me.

I swim standing up and I may be slow
But that never stops me having a go.
I'm the best baby seahorse you ever did see.
Like I said before, I love being me!

My tummy's round and I bob up and down
And I'm the size of a cup of tea!
I like to hold on to a seaweed frond
And take a rest frequentlee-ee . . .

I can wiggle my nose around and around
And look with my eyes, both up and down.
I'm a bright spark, clever lad, diddlee-dee
I will tell you again that I love being me,
I love being me, I love being meeeeeeee!
(That's right!)

Glide through the water like a sea**horse**, rocking forward and back.

Kneel down and bring one foot forward so your knee is up. Lift your arms above your head.

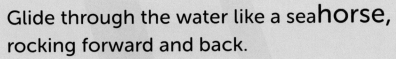

Rock forward, bending your back and lifting your heart to the sky. Straighten up as you rock back.

Neigh! Neigh!

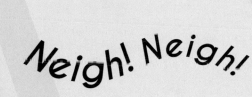

Keep rocking forward and back, making a neighing noise.

To be Norris on your other side, lift up your back knee and stand up. Turn the other way and drop down onto the other knee.

It's great to meet Norris. We are going to be good friends and have lots of fun in this wonderful underwater world. We **twirl** together in a flurry of happy bubbles.

To twirl with Norris, stand up tall, legs wide and arms out to the side.

Twirl your arms one way and then the other so you start to spin. Keep your feet on the ground.

Norris tells us he's very excited because he has been invited to join The Best Fish In The Sea Club. Norris has never heard of this club before, but it's called The Best Fish In The Sea Club, so it must be the best . . . mustn't it?

The club's first meet-up is at the Coral Reef Café today. We have to leave! It's already late and Norris can only swim very slowly.

On our way we pass one of Norris's best friends, Mimi the **mermaid**.

Swish your legs like a mermaid's tail. Sit on your bottom, with your legs out long in front of you.

Then bend your legs round to the side. Put one hand on your knee. The other hand is behind you on the ground.

Sit up tall and twist round to look over your shoulder.

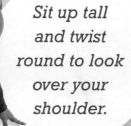

Mimi says, "Bon chance, petit Norris", which means "Good luck, little Norris" in French.

Then she swishes her tail around the other way and blows him a special mermaid kiss.

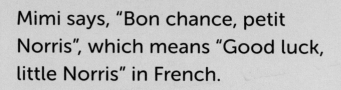

Look to the front again and say, "Oo la la!" Can you blow Norris a kiss?

Then try swishing your mermaid tail to the other side!

Look to the front and stretch your legs out straight. Then bend your legs round to the other side.

Put one hand on your knee, the other hand behind you and twist around to look over your shoulder.

17

Coral Reef Café

At last we get to the Coral Reef Café. The other members of the club are already there. When they see Norris they don't look very happy.

A tough-looking little **crab** scuttles over.

He says, "Oy you, big nose! You can't be in The Best Fish In The Sea Club because your nose is too big. And if you do join . . . I will pinch you on the nose with my crab claws!"

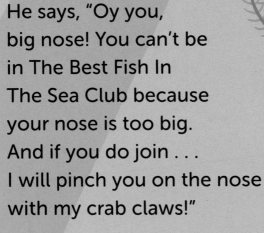

Then he scuttles away.

Poor Norris! He feels a bit upset by that! He loves his nose. But he does not want to make a fuss so he decides not to say anything.

Be a little scuttling crab. Sit on your bottom and bend your knees, keeping your feet flat on the ground.

Place your hands behind you with your fingers pointing toward your bottom.

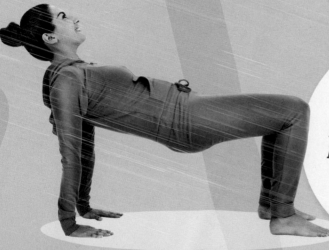

Press your feet and hands into the ground and lift your hips to the sky. Move sideways saying, "Digga, digga, digga!"

Digga digga digga!

Scuttle sideways like a crab in the other direction.

19

Next a pair of unfriendly **wolf fish** come over.

They say, "All right, big nose! You can join the club if you can make yourself look like a tree."

They want to make Norris look silly.

21

But Norris is quite pleased because he's good at tree pose. He stands up and does his best **tree**.

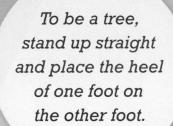

To be a tree, stand up straight and place the heel of one foot on the other foot.

Bring your hands together at your heart.

Grow your branches into the sky. Can you stand tall and count to 10?

Norris is great at tree pose. He even shows the nasty wolf fish he can do it on the other side.

Stand up straight and place the other heel on your foot. Breathe slowly and count to 10.

As you get good at balancing, try moving your foot up your leg, below your knee.

If your tree is really strong, you can raise your foot up your leg to your thigh.

23

The nasty wolf fish just laugh at him!

Hahaha!

"Only joking, haha! You can't join
The Best Fish In The Sea Club
because you have a big, silly,
round tummy! HAHAHA!"

Poor Norris!

That's not very nice at all.

Become a wolf fish again! Press your hands and feet into the ground and lift your bottom to the sky.

Then come down to your knees and lie on your tummy. Place your hands under your shoulders and lift your mean wolf fish chest!

The wolf fish have gone, still laughing loudly,
and now a **shark** is coming over.

She swims right up to Norris and says, "Err? Excuse me . . .
My name's Shona. Just wanted to let you know that you
can't join The Best Fish In The Sea Club. The wolf fish and
crab said that you are a really bad swimmer. If that's true,
you definitely can't join! Sorry! Okay, see ya."

Shona swims off back to the mean wolf fish and
the tough crab.

DUH duh . . .

DUH duh . . .

DUH duh DUH duh DUH duh!

Swim like a shark. Lie on your front with your legs stretched out.

Criss-cross your fingers behind your back and lift your arms up like a shark's fin.

Rock from side to side making shark noises.

DUH, duh, DUH, duh!

This is awful. Norris needs to get away from these bullies.
We help him find a nice oyster **shell** to curl up in.

The bullies have made poor Norris feel really bad.
They are not very nice and they are making others
gang up on him too.

This is not The Best Fish In The Sea Club,
it's The WORST Fish In The Sea Club!
All of these horrible animals are bullying Norris.

That's not right!

Sit on your bottom and bend your knees so the soles of your feet touch.

Hold your feet and fold your body forward to close your shell.

When this sort of thing happens it helps to speak to a wise, grown-up friend . . .

29

. . . and here come just the friends Norris needs.

Here's Tommy the **turtle**.

Turn into a turtle. Open your legs wide and bend your knees a little. Put your hands on the floor between your feet.

Slide your hands and arms under your legs and flatten your body down to the floor.

Slap your hands on the floor to flap your flippers.

Slap, slap, slap!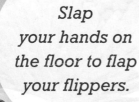

30

And here's Squish the **fish**.

Float like a fish. Sit up with legs stretched and toes pointed.

Gently lie back on your elbows. Then pop your chest out – pop, pop, pop! – and look to the sky.

Keep your elbows under your shoulders and hold the sides of your bottom as you pop your chest. Look up to the sky but don't hang your head back.

Tommy and Squish are worried when they see Norris all huddled up in a sad little **ball** inside the shell.

Make yourself into a little ball. Sit on your bottom and hug your knees. Tuck your chin down.

Tommy asks Norris, "Why the long face?" Norris explains. "Well, I wanted to join The Best Fish In The Sea Club, but they said that I can't because my nose is too long and I have a big, round tummy and I'm not a very fast swimmer."

Tommy the turtle thinks this is awful.

Turn into a turtle. Open your legs wide and bend your knees a little. Put your hands on the floor between your feet.

Slide your hands and arms under your legs and flatten your body down to the ground.

Tommy shakes his head slowly and says, "Oh Norris, don't listen to them! You are a wonderful seahorse. What do you think about the mean things they said?"

Norris sits up and uncurls his tail.

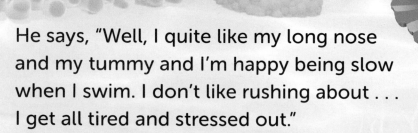

Sit up tall and stretch your legs out in front of you.

He says, "Well, I quite like my long nose and my tummy and I'm happy being slow when I swim. I don't like rushing about . . . I get all tired and stressed out."

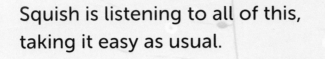

Squish is listening to all of this, taking it easy as usual.

Point your toes, lie back on your elbows and pop your chest out. Look to the sky. Pop, pop, pop!

Squish says, "You are so right, Norris! You must not listen to them. They are bullying you. You don't need to change anything . . . and you certainly don't need to join their club. In fact . . . why don't you start your own club?"

Sit up with your legs crossed.

Be a happy seahorse! Come onto your knees and step one foot forward. Lift your arms above your head.

Then start to rock forward and back.

Norris loves this idea. "Yes!!!" he shouts. "I'm going to start my own club."

"I'm going to call it the I Love Being Me Club and anyone can join . . . no matter what they look like or how fast they swim! You have just got to be nice in the I Love Being Me Club!"

This is more like it. Norris has a smile back on his face.

Uh oh! Shona the shark is coming over again.

Swim like Shona! Lie on your tummy. Criss-cross your fingers behind your back and lift your fin.

Rock from side to side making shark noises, "DUH duh, DUH, duh!"

Shona says, "Err . . . excuse me . . . do you remember me? I'm Shona the shark. I just heard you talking about the I Love Being Me Club. Do you think . . . Could I ask you . . . Can I join? I'm really fed up with that other club. I don't like those guys telling me what to do and what to say. I don't like it at all."

Norris is delighted.

"Yes, Shona!" he says. "Of course you can join! You are very welcome."

Be a happy seahorse! Come onto your knees and bend the other leg in front. Lift your arms above your head and rock forward and back.

Soon all of the animals and creatures from The Best Fish In The Sea Club start to join the I Love Being Me Club.

Norris has done it! He has started his own club and everybody wants to join him!

Now that all is well with our friend Norris, it's time for us to say goodbye and **swim** home.

Kneel with your hands down by your side.

Rise up on your knees, breathing in as you lift your arms out to the side and above your head.

Breathe out as you bring your arms down and sit back on your heels. Do this 3 times.

When we reach the beach, we find Bez the blue-footed booby waiting for us.

Stand up and fold forward like Bez, with your wings pointing down to the ground.

Float your wings out to your sides and then back down to the ground. Keep the movement gentle and steady. Repeat 3 times.

We have had a busy time. So we lie on Bez's comfy back, all cosy in his warm feathers.

As we relax, let's think about our amazing adventure with Norris.

Lie down comfortably on your back, your feet apart and your arms a little away from your sides.

Feel your arms and legs become heavy and long. Melt into the ground and close your eyes to enjoy a rest and think about the yoga adventure you have been on.

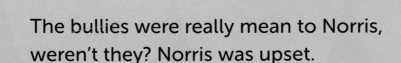

The bullies were really mean to Norris, weren't they? Norris was upset.

Bullying is never okay. If it happens – and it might happen to you or a friend, or you might see it happen to someone else – you must always tell a grown-up. Don't worry about being a telltale. You are not, you are helping!

That bully probably needs help too. Bullies sometimes do mean things because they feel weak inside. They need to feel strong by saying horrible things about other people and making them feel bad.

Ignore the bully and walk away as calmly as you can. You always have friends – and can find new friends – who think you are great just as you are. Enjoy being with your friends and you will feel strong.

This is an affirmation. Affirmations are good and helpful thoughts that we say out loud.

When we say an affirmation, we make it come alive – like planting a seed and giving it sunshine and water. Then it grows into something big and strong that will help us in our life.

Thoughts can be very powerful things. When we turn them into affirmations they become even stronger..

As you lie on the floor, put one hand on your chest and one hand on your tummy and try saying the affirmation out loud.

Believe the words as you say them and they will grow stronger and stronger, until they are part of who you are.

Repeat the words a few times out loud. It doesn't have to be more than a whisper.

"I love being me!"

"I am strong!"

Norris also likes this affirmation. You can copy him or make up some good ones of your own.

We rest quietly in this peaceful time.
We are so pleased for Norris.
We love the I Love Being Me Club –
it sounds like a lot of fun!

It's time to end our yoga adventure,
so let's sit up like we did at the beginning.

*Did you find Coco the crab
hiding in every picture?*

Slowly start to wiggle your fingers and toes. Have a little stretch and then roll over to one side. Sit up slowly and cross your legs.

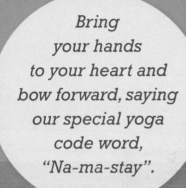

Bring your hands to your heart and bow forward, saying our special yoga code word, "Na-ma-stay".

Namaste!
Goodbye!

Jaime's top tips for using the Cosmic Kids books

Grown-ups, here are a few tips for helping children get the most out of the Cosmic Kids adventure books. It doesn't matter if you don't practise yoga yourself, you can still encourage your children to have a go at the poses – and you might want to have some fun trying them out for yourself!

Read the story, copy the moves and enjoy the adventure

This is an active book that encourages children to act out the story by doing the yoga moves. It's a lot of fun and provides children with a great, balanced yoga routine. They can come back to the book again and again, becoming more skilled and eventually developing their own yoga practice. After going on the yoga adventure a few times, they may even be able to do the whole routine, with all the poses in order, without looking at the book!

Start by reading the story and looking at the pictures

Being able to visualize the characters and understand what's happening in the story will help children as they try out the yoga moves.

Use a yoga mat (or a towel)

A yoga mat gives a soft surface to lie on, as well as a defined space to practise in. Plus it makes it feel like 'proper' yoga! If you don't have a mat, try using a rug or a big towel.

Taking part is more important than getting it right

Even though all the yoga poses in the book are adapted from traditional 'adult' yoga, the key is to make the experience as fun and playful for children as possible. So rather than stopping them to correct their poses, it's best to let the children interpret what they see and read and have fun making the shapes of the poses. With practice, as they re-read and look at the pictures again, they will become more accurate. The main goal is for them to enjoy the yoga!

Try to do each pose on both sides

This helps to keep the body in balance.

Join in to help the kids get the most out of their yoga adventure

- Make the animal noises! Encouraging the children to make fun sounds while they do the moves helps remind them of the poses.
- Get the children to come up with extra ideas for the story. You could ask them what the tough little crab is called, for example, or where the wolf fish live.
- Bring the poses into everyday life. It's always a good time for a twirl! Or you might want to be a mermaid, crawl like a crab or swim like a shark . . .

Talk about the story

Each Cosmic Kids adventure offers practical advice for dealing with a particular issue. It's really useful to talk to your children about what they learned from the story so they have some ideas and techniques available when similar situations occur in real life. Ask if they can relate to any of the characters in the story and what they would do if something like that happened to them. Norris shows how to stand up to bullies by being calm and confident, and loving ourselves for who we are – even if we're not the fastest swimmers in the sea. Norris also finds strength by talking to wise friends.

Practise the affirmations

These short statements are handy tools for daily life, helping to provide instant calm and also to sow the seeds for positive change (see pages 42–3).

Try out the video

You can watch and practise with me on the Cosmic Kids YouTube channel – access Norris's adventure and many others via my website: www.cosmickids.com

Watch out for more Cosmic Kids books . . .

There are lots more yoga adventures to be had. You can travel to Africa and help Lulu the lion cub learn to roar. In the Wild West, Sheriff Updown the rabbit is in a spot of bother with the bandits – can his amazing Zappy Happy save the day? And Twilight the unicorn needs a hand delivering starshine to the magical Land of Sleep.

For Martin, Mini and Spence – and Cosmic Kids all over the world

Author acknowledgments

A huge thank you to Konrad Welz, Nick Hilditch and my super-talented husband Martin for the amazing work done behind the scenes at Cosmic Kids. Thank you so much Fiona Robertson, Jade Wheaton, Simona Sideri and the team at Watkins Publishing for getting behind these books and working hard to make them brilliant. Thank you David Lloyd, for taking such good photos. Thank you to teachers, parents and especially kids who have given me the inspiration to make these stories, and to our partnership team at YouTube for helping us keep Cosmic Kids yoga freely available to kids all over the world.

About Cosmic Kids

Jaime and Martin Amor are a husband-and-wife team from Henley-on-Thames who run Cosmic Kids with the aim of making yoga and mindfulness fun for kids. It all began in their local village hall in 2012, when they filmed a 'yoga adventure' Jaime had been sharing in her yoga classes in nearby schools. This was the first of many videos posted to YouTube and now – many monthly episodes later – millions of kids worldwide have discovered yoga and mindfulness through the free videos. Every Cosmic Kids yoga adventure is written to help kids learn a simple lesson for a happy life, so that they understand themselves and the world around them a little better.

To have more fun with Cosmic Kids, visit **cosmickids.com**!

Norris the Seahorse Takes on the Bullies
Jaime Amor

First published in the UK and USA in 2016 by
Watkins, an imprint of Watkins Media Limited
19 Cecil Court
London WC2N 4EZ

enquiries@watkinspublishing.com

Publisher: Jo Lal
Development Editor: Fiona Robertson
Editor: Simona Sideri
Head of Design: Viki Ottewill
Designer and Picture Research: Jade Wheaton
Production: Uzma Taj
Commissioned Illustration: Nick Hilditch
Commissioned Photography: Evolve Portraits

A CIP record for this book is available from the British Library

ISBN: 978-1-78028-956-4

10 9 8 7 6 5 4 3 2 1

Typeset in Museo Sans Rounded, Rockwell and Caviar Dreams
Colour reproduction by XY Digital, UK
Printed in China

www.watkinspublishing.com